BUTTERFLY STORY

Anca Hariton

DUTTON CHILDREN'S BOOKS   NEW YORK

ACKNOWLEDGMENTS

I would like to deeply thank

Don Miller, Professor of Entomology, University of California at Berkeley
Alvin F. Ludke, Entomologist, Marine World Africa USA
John Staples, Breeder of Lepidoptera, Nature Discoveries
Norman Penny, Entomologist, the Academy of Sciences, San Francisco
Arlyn Christopherson, Director of Education, the Oakland Zoo
Stevanne Auerbach, Director, Butterfly Lovers International

for their generous professional guidance.

Library of Congress Cataloging-in-Publication Data

Hariton, Anca.
Butterfly story/written and illustrated by Anca Hariton.—1st ed.
p.   cm.
ISBN 0-525-45212-5
1. Butterflies—Life cycles—Juvenile literature.
2. Butterflies—Juvenile literature.   [1. Butterflies.   2. Caterpillars.]   I. Title.
QL544.2.H37   1995   595.78′9—dc20   94-19377   CIP   AC

Published in the United States 1995
by Dutton Children's Books, a division of Penguin USA
375 Hudson Street, New York, New York 10014
Designed by Amy Berniker
Printed in Hong Kong
First Edition
1 3 5 7 9 10 8 6 4 2

For all those who dare to live on fragile but masterful wings.
To Marianne Rothe, our faithful friend who showed me the way,
and to my husband, Florentin Cristian,
who taught me the wisdom of flying.

A.H.

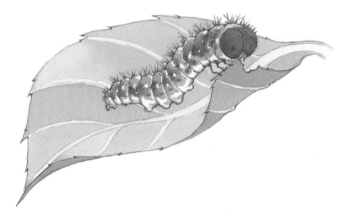

It is springtime in the pasture. Birds chirp and frogs croak by the stream. A butterfly flies with the breeze. It has bright red stripes on its dark wings.

The butterfly lands on a stinging nettle bush.

It lays one tiny green egg on a nettle leaf. Then it flies to another bush.

The egg sticks to the leaf, even in the wind and rain.

Inside the egg is a little caterpillar. After a week it begins to move. It munches at the ribbed eggshell and splits the shell open.

Then it crawls out.

The tiny caterpillar is hungry. It needs to eat. *Crunch, crunch*. It chews the fresh green leaf. Its body is soft and fuzzy, with fourteen stumpy legs. To move, it pulls itself up into a loop and then pushes its long body over the leaf.

The caterpillar spins a silky thread that looks like a shiny trail behind it.

Crunch, crunch. Five days later the caterpillar has eaten so much it is too big for its skin. It wriggles and finally splits its tight skin open. Then it crawls out. It puffs itself up with air and fills every fold of its stretchy new skin. The caterpillar grows wider and longer. Now it is hungry again.

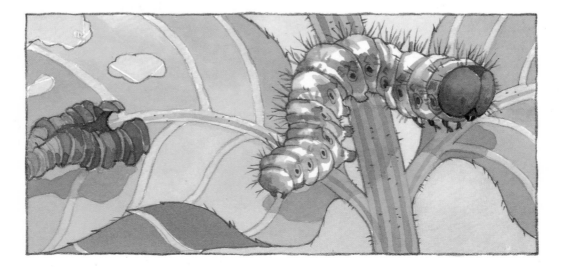

Crunch, crunch. The caterpillar can't stop eating. After ten days it has eaten so much and grown so big that its skin is too tight again. The caterpillar sheds its old skin again. It grows some more. During the next week and a half, the caterpillar outgrows its tight skin two more times.

A bird chirps. It swoops down to eat the juicy caterpillar. But the caterpillar quickly drops into the leaves below by means of its silky thread.

It uses this fine thread like a rescue rope to crawl back up when the bird is gone and it is safe to return.

When it is three weeks old, the caterpillar is full grown and about as big as your toe. Now the caterpillar stops eating.

Deep in the branches of the nettle bush, the caterpillar weaves a small sticky bed on the back of a leaf. It clings to this bed with the back of its body and hangs with its head down.

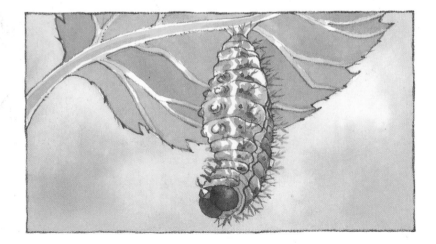

One last time the caterpillar shakes itself and sheds its old skin.
But this time, the caterpillar's new skin is different. It is tight and stiff.

It is called a pupa now.

For two weeks the hard pupa does not move. It looks like a shriveled leaf.

But the dull pupa case is a hiding place. Inside it, the caterpillar is changing.

After two weeks the pupa twitches. Its skin cracks open. Something wet and plump crawls out. It has wings folded tightly on its back like a pack. It takes its first breath and drops some waste.

Then it pushes a special juice from its body into the veins of its wings. Slowly, the red striped wings unfold. They grow bigger and bigger while the body that carries them gets lighter and lighter.

A butterfly is born.

In one hour, the juice that fills the veins of its four wings will harden. The butterfly has to stretch its wings all the way out by then. Otherwise the wings will dry folded, and the butterfly will not be able to fly. *Whoosh, whoosh.* The butterfly moves its wings up and down. They bend in the wind but do not break.

Then the butterfly spreads its wings and takes off. It dives and sails
in the breeze like a living kite.

Colorful powdery scales cover the wings like tiny feathers. They help the butterfly glide smoothly. They also give the wings their bright colors.

The butterfly has a hard head with two long feelers. The upper part of its body is strong and stiff, like its pupa case was. The lower part of its body is soft and fuzzy, like it was as a caterpillar.

The butterfly lands on a flower. It uncoils its tongue, which is used like a straw to sip the flower's sweet nectar.

One week has passed. The butterfly soars above the trees. Another red striped butterfly follows it.

Late in the afternoon, the butterfly comes back to the stinging nettle bush. Carefully it lays one tiny green egg on a leaf.

In the pasture the birds chirp, the frogs croak, and the butterfly flies away with the breeze.

BUTTERFLIES AND MOTHS are members of the *Lepidoptera* order of insects. The butterfly shown in this book is a red admiral butterfly (*Vanessa atalanta*) of the *Nymphalidae*, or brush-footed, family of butterflies. It can be found in many parts of the world, including North America, Europe, New Zealand, northern Africa, and Asia.

Like all butterflies and many other insects, the red admiral butterfly develops in four stages. The process of this dramatic transformation is known as "complete metamorphosis." Metamorphosis begins when the female red admiral butterfly lays a small, single egg on a leaf of the nettle bush.

As it hatches from the egg, the red admiral caterpillar often eats part of the egg's nutritious shell, and then it begins to eat the nettle leaf. While it eats, the caterpillar may draw the edges of the leaf together with a silky thread—forming a tiny, protective "tent" around itself.

The caterpillar's flexible body has thirteen segments and fourteen legs. The hard legs on the front segments are used for gripping. The middle segments have soft, fleshy legs with tiny suction cup–like ends. The last segment has a pair of clasps that keeps the back end of its body attached to leaves while the front end is moving.

The caterpillar does not have a skeleton inside its body. Its skin is considered a kind of "exoskeleton," or exterior skeleton. In order to grow, the caterpillar pops open its old skin by puffing itself up with air, allowing the newer, larger skin underneath to come to the surface. This is why a caterpillar seems to grow suddenly each time it sheds its old skin.

The pupa that forms around the caterpillar as it begins its transformation into a butterfly is also called a chrysalis. By the time the butterfly is ready to hatch, the pupa has become translucent. You can even see the pattern of the butterfly's wings through it.

The butterfly that emerges from the pupa is very different from the caterpillar it once was. It has four wings covered with tiny colored scales that give the butterfly its distinctive markings. Instead of the caterpillar's simple eyes that could only tell dark from light, the butterfly now has complex eyes that can see colors and motion. Instead of jaws for chewing, the butterfly has a coiled tongue for sipping nectar from flowers, which is how it eats. Instead of fourteen stumpy legs, the butterfly has three pairs of legs. The short front pair, called its brush feet, are covered with sensory hairs and are useless for walking but helpful for locating food. On its head, the butterfly has two delicate antennae that can bend, touch, and smell, helping the butterfly to find food or sense the direction of the wind.

You are most likely to spot the red admiral (and other butterflies) on a dry and sunny day. Its big, shimmering, colorful wings make it an especially strong flier and a beautiful and memorable sight.